# Sherlock Holmes and The Hasty Holiday

Mabel Swift

Sherlock Holmes and The Hasty Holiday

(A Sherlock Holmes Mystery - Book 3)

By

Mabel Swift

Copyright 2024 by Mabel Swift



This is a work of fiction and any resemblance to any person living or dead is purely coincidental.

# Contents

# Chapter 1

It was early afternoon, and inside 221B Baker Street, Sherlock Holmes and Dr John Watson relaxed in their respective armchairs, enjoying a brief respite from the bustling streets of London. Holmes, his eyes closed in contemplation, gently plucked at the strings of his violin, while Watson perused the pages of the latest medical journal, occasionally making notes in the margins.

Their tranquil moment was interrupted by a sharp knock at the door. Mrs Hudson, their landlady, poked her head into the room. "Mr Holmes, there's a Mrs Agnes Fairfax here to see you. She seems quite distressed."

Holmes's eyes snapped open, and he set aside his violin. "Send her in, Mrs Hudson."

A moment later, a woman in her early thirties entered the room. She was dressed in a fashionable, though slightly travel-worn, ensemble, and her face bore the unmistakable signs of worry and fatigue.

"Mr Holmes, Dr Watson," she began, her voice trembling slightly, "I apologise for the intrusion, but I desperately need your help."

Watson rose from his chair, offering the woman a seat. "Please, Mrs Fairfax, sit down and tell us what troubles you."

As she settled into the proffered chair, Mrs Fairfax took a deep breath to compose herself. "It's my younger sister, Dorothy Davenport. She's gone missing." She paused, as if struggling to find the next words. "Well, not missing, I don't suppose. But she has left London suddenly in peculiar circumstances, and I fear something dreadful may have happened to her."

Holmes said, "Please, Mrs Fairfax, start from the beginning. When did you last see your sister?"

Mrs Fairfax explained, "Dorothy and I have a standing arrangement to meet for lunch on the first Saturday of every month, which is today, of course. I live in Birmingham with my husband and children, while Dorothy resides here in London. She works as a social secretary for Lord and Lady Cavendish. These monthly meetings for lunch are a cherished tradition for us both."

Watson nodded sympathetically. "And she failed to arrive for your scheduled lunch today?"

Mrs Fairfax continued, "She did, but I already knew she wasn't going to be there. Two days ago, I received a telegram from Dorothy, sent from a village in Devon. She said she'd won a competition for a two-week holiday there and wouldn't be able to make our monthly meeting."

Holmes's eyebrows rose slightly. "And this struck you as unusual?"

"Highly unusual, Mr Holmes. Dorothy is not one for spontaneous trips or entering competitions, as far as I am aware. She's always been the sensible, reliable sort. I sent a return message to make sure she was okay, and to ask why she hadn't told me of her holiday earlier. She answered my telegram with a very brief note saying she was fine and I was not to worry. No explanation was given about the sudden trip away. Well, my imagination ran riot, and I imagined Dorothy had been kidnapped, or she had been lured to that village in Devon because some terrible fate awaited her. I was all for travelling down to Devon, despite the long journey, but my husband said Dorothy was most likely taking a break from the stresses of her job. But I couldn't shake the feeling that something was wrong, so I contacted the police." She stopped talking and her mouth set in a firm line.

"And what did the police tell you?" Watson prompted gently.

With a hint of annoyance in her voice, Mrs Fairfax replied, "They treated me like a hysterical woman who had nothing better to do with her time than worry about her sister. They agreed with what my husband said, and that Dorothy was most likely having a restful holiday and the last thing she needed, was a visit from the police to check up on her."

Sherlock frowned. "I assume you emphasised how concerned you were, Mrs Fairfax?"

"I most certainly did, Mr Holmes." Her grip on her handbag tightened. "But they didn't take me seriously, not at all. And that's why I came here. I only wished I'd have come here sooner. Goodness knows what may have happened to Dorothy because of my delay."

Holmes said gently, "Tell me, Mrs Fairfax, does your sister have any reason to fear for her safety? Has she mentioned any troubling incidents or individuals in her life recently?"

Mrs Fairfax shook her head. "No, nothing of the sort. Dorothy is well-liked by all who know her. She's kind, considerate, and utterly devoted to her work with the Cavendishes. I can't imagine anyone wishing her harm."

Watson frowned thoughtfully. "And you're certain she sent the telegram herself? Could someone else have sent it in her name?"

"Oh! I never thought of that. I suppose it's possible," Mrs Fairfax admitted, "but who would do such a thing? And why?"

Holmes said, "Mrs Fairfax, I understand your concern for your sister's well-being. While it is entirely possible that she did, indeed, win a holiday and took advantage of the opportunity for a rest, your instincts should not be dismissed. Watson and I will look into the matter and see if we can uncover any information regarding your sister's whereabouts and the circumstances surrounding her sudden departure."

Relief washed over Mrs Fairfax's face. "Thank you, Mr Holmes. I cannot tell you how much this means to me. I just want to know that Dorothy is safe and well."

Watson offered the woman a reassuring smile. "We will do our utmost to locate your sister, Mrs Fairfax. In the meantime, if you can provide us with any additional information—her address here in London, her place of employment, and the names of any close friends or acquaintances—it would be most helpful."

Sherlock added, "And may we take those telegrams your sister sent you? Has she given the address of where she is staying in Devon?"

Mrs Fairfax nodded. "She has, and it is a blessing to know that. Unless it's a fake address." Tears sprang to her eyes. "I cannot stop thinking the worst about her, no matter how hard I try."

Dr Watson handed her a handkerchief and said, "I understand your concern, really I do. We will deal with this matter with utmost urgency. You have my word."

Sherlock added his agreement, smiling kindly at the distraught woman.

Mrs Fairfax dabbed at her eyes and composed herself. She handed the telegrams to Sherlock and then gave the requested information about Dorothy to Dr Watson.

Once they had everything they needed, Sherlock said, "Where might we contact you, Mrs Fairfax?"

Mrs Fairfax replied, "I wish I could stay in London longer, but I have to return to Birmingham to look after my children. I suspect my husband is already at his wits' end after looking after the little ones in my absence. Could you contact me by telegram, please? I'll give you the address of my nearest telegram office. I shall call in there often to look for any messages from you." She smiled sadly. "I suppose I could wait for telegrams to be delivered to my house as normal, but I am so worried..." Fresh tears came to her eyes.

Sherlock held up his hand. "There is no need to explain your worries, Mrs Fairfax. I will ensure that regular telegrams are sent to you. We will make some enquiries locally today and see what information we can uncover about your sister's disappearance. We will also journey to Devon and meet her in person."

"You will?" Mrs Fairfax asked.

"We will," Sherlock confirmed. He smiled gently. "Now, is there anything else you wish us to know? Or anything you need from us?"

Mrs Fairfax stood. "I can't think of anything else." She smiled at them. "Thank you so much, Mr Holmes, Dr Watson. I already feel a little better by knowing you are helping me."

Dr Watson escorted Mrs Agnes Fairfax out of the room and down the stairs. Sherlock heard his reassuring words to her drifting up the steps.

Once Mrs Fairfax had left the building, Dr Watson returned to the living room and said, "Well, Holmes, what do you make of this?"

Sherlock replied, "I believe we have a most intriguing case on our hands. While Mrs Fairfax's concerns may prove unfounded, there is something about this sudden disappearance that doesn't sit right."

Watson nodded in agreement. Concern filled his face. "Let us hope that this mystery has a happy resolution for all involved."

# Chapter 2

Sherlock glanced out of the window and saw Mrs Fairfax walking along the street, dabbing at her eyes. He said, "Watson, we must waste no time. Our first stop shall be the boarding house where Miss Davenport resides. Perhaps there, we may uncover some clues as to her sudden disappearance."

Watson nodded in agreement, already reaching for his hat and coat.

The two men set off through the bustling streets of London, their strides purposeful and their minds focused on the task at hand. It wasn't long before they arrived at the boarding house where Dorothy Davenport lived, a well-maintained building with a modest but respectable exterior.

Holmes rapped sharply on the door, and moments later, it swung open to reveal a woman in her late fifties. Her greying hair was pulled back into a neat bun, and her keen eyes regarded the visitors with a mixture of suspicion and curiosity.

"Good afternoon, madam," Holmes greeted, tipping his hat. "I am Sherlock Holmes, and this is my associate, Dr John Watson. Are you Mrs Olive King, the proprietress of this establishment?"

The woman's gaze narrowed slightly, but she nodded. "I am. And what brings you gentlemen to my door?"

"We were hoping to speak with you about one of your lodgers, a Miss Dorothy Davenport," Holmes explained.

Mrs King's suspicion seemed to deepen at the mention of Dorothy's name. "And what, pray tell, is your interest in Miss Davenport?"

Watson stepped forward, his kind face and gentle demeanour serving to put the landlady slightly more at ease. "We've been engaged by Miss Davenport's sister, Mrs Agnes Fairfax, who is deeply concerned about her well-being."

After a moment's hesitation, Mrs King stepped aside, allowing the two men to enter. "Very well. Come into the parlour, and we can discuss this further."

Once settled in the modest but well-appointed room, Holmes began, "Mrs King, we understand that Miss Davenport recently departed on a sudden holiday. Her sister found this behaviour quite out of character and has asked us to look into the matter."

Mrs King sighed, her hands folded primly in her lap. "I must admit, I was surprised myself when Miss Davenport informed me of her plans. It was most unlike her to make such a decision on a whim."

Watson nodded. "And did she give any indication as to where she was going or how long she intended to be away?"

"She mentioned having won a holiday to Devon, to a village called Clovelly, I believe. Said she'd be gone for two weeks." Mrs King paused, a thoughtful expression crossing her face. "But you know, even though it was unexpected, I wasn't overly concerned. Miss Davenport is a sensible woman. I have no doubt she'll return safely when her holiday is through."

Holmes asked, "And did you notice anything unusual about her behaviour in the days leading up to her departure? Any changes in routine or demeanour?"

Mrs King considered the question for a moment. "No, not really. She seemed her usual self."

Holmes took a moment's pause to ask his next question. "Did Miss Davenport have any unusual visitors recently? Or any letters that may have caused her some concern?"

"The only letter she received was the one informing her about that holiday, not that I saw it," Mrs King replied. "As for any unusual visitors, no, she didn't. She seldom receives any visitors at all."

Holmes rose from his seat, "Mrs King, I think it would be most helpful if we could take a look at Miss Davenport's room. It may hold some clues as to her state of mind before her departure."

Mrs King's eyes widened at Sherlock's request, her expression shifting from one of polite concern to outright indignation. "I beg your pardon, Mr Holmes," she said, her voice rising slightly, "but I absolutely cannot allow you or Dr Watson to enter Miss Davenport's room. It is strictly against the rules of this establishment for males to enter the rooms of my tenants."

Sherlock said, "Mrs King, I assure you that our intentions are purely investigative. We have no desire to compromise the reputation of your boarding house or to cause any discomfort to your other lodgers."

But the landlady was having none of it. She rose from her seat, her posture rigid and her face set in a stern expression. "Mr Holmes, I have run this boarding house for many years, and I have done so by maintaining a strict code of conduct. No men, under any circumstances, are permitted to enter the private rooms of my lodgers, and that is that. I must insist that you respect my rules."

Watson, sensing the rising tension, attempted to intervene. "Mrs King, we do apologise for any offence. We certainly don't wish to cause any trouble."

Mrs King turned her steely gaze upon the doctor. "Dr Watson, while I appreciate your apology, I'm afraid my decision is final. I must ask you and Mr Holmes to leave now. I have nothing further to say on the matter, and I no longer wish to discuss Miss Davenport's private life with you."

Sherlock, realising that further persuasion would be futile, said, "Very well, Mrs King. We shall take our leave. Thank you for your time."

With that, the two men made their way out of the boarding house, the door closing firmly behind them. Once on the path outside, Sherlock turned to Watson, a thoughtful expression on his face.

"It seems we've reached an impasse, Watson," he said, his eyes narrowing slightly. "Mrs King is clearly a formidable woman, and her dedication to her rules is admirable, if somewhat inconvenient for our purposes."

Watson nodded, his brow furrowed. "Indeed, Holmes. But where does that leave us? If we can't access Miss Dav-

enport's room, how are we to proceed with our investigation?"

Sherlock replied, "Fear not, my dear Watson. I have a
solution in mind. We shall need to enlist the help of someone who can navigate the inner workings of the boarding
house without any objections from Mrs King."

"Who did you have in mind, Holmes?"

Sherlock smiled. "I know just the person. And so do
you."

# Chapter 3

Sherlock Holmes and Dr John Watson returned to 221B Baker Street. Upon entering the building, Sherlock immediately sought out Mrs Hudson, their loyal and ever-helpful landlady. He found her in the kitchen, preparing a pot of tea for her tenants.

"Ah, Mrs Hudson," Sherlock said, his voice tinged with urgency. "I wonder if I might have a word with you about a most pressing matter. We need your help with our present investigation."

Mrs Hudson looked up from her task. "Of course, Mr Holmes. What seems to be the trouble?"

Sherlock proceeded to explain the details of the case, recounting their visit to Mrs King's boarding house and the stern rebuff they had received when requesting access to Miss Davenport's room.

"You see, Mrs Hudson," Sherlock continued, "it is imperative that we gain entry to Miss Davenport's quarters.

There may be vital clues within that could shed light on her abrupt departure and the reasons behind it. At this stage, we don't know if the supposed holiday is real, or if there is something more sinister at play."

Mrs Hudson listened intently, her brow furrowed in thought. "And you believe that Mrs King would be more amenable to granting me access, despite what she said to you about not wanting to discuss Dorothy's private life any further?"

Sherlock nodded, a glimmer of hope in his eyes. "Precisely. Mrs King may be more inclined to trust a fellow woman in this delicate matter."

Mrs Hudson smiled. "Well, Mr Holmes, I would be delighted to assist you in your investigation. I've known Olive for many years, and despite her gruff exterior, I'm certain she'll see the wisdom in allowing me to take a peek into Miss Davenport's room."

Watson, who had been listening intently to the conversation, reached into his pocket and retrieved one of his small, leather-bound notebooks. He handed it to Mrs Hudson with a grateful smile.

"Here, Mrs Hudson," he said, "please take this notebook. If you should come across anything of interest in

Miss Davenport's room, you can jot down your observations. Your keen eye for detail may prove invaluable."

Mrs Hudson accepted the notebook with a nod. "I shall do my very best, Dr Watson. You can count on me to be thorough in my examination."

With that, Mrs Hudson bustled out of the kitchen, a determined spring in her step. Sherlock and Watson watched her go, a sense of relief washing over them.

"I do believe we've made the right choice in enlisting Mrs Hudson's aid," Sherlock said. "And while we wait for her return, I suggest we discuss Dorothy's case further."

"Excellent idea. I'll pour some tea and bring it up."

Minutes later, Holmes and Watson were ensconced in their familiar armchairs, the crackling fire in the hearth casting a warm glow upon their pensive faces.

Watson said, "So Holmes, what are your thoughts regarding Miss Davenport's abrupt departure?"

Sherlock answered, "There are several theories that come to mind. The first, and perhaps most obvious, is that Miss Davenport has won a holiday and simply neglected to inform her sister of her prize when she was first notified of it. However, given the close relationship between the two, as described by Mrs Fairfax, this seems unlikely."

Watson nodded. "What other explanations have you considered, Holmes?"

"The second possibility is that Miss Davenport has been lured away under false pretences. Perhaps someone has used the guise of a holiday competition to entice her to Devon, with odious intentions in mind. A possibility that has already occurred to Mrs Fairfax and is causing her a great deal of concern."

Watson sighed. "Yes, I agree with your thoughts on that point. But who would wish to harm Miss Davenport? From what we have gathered so far, she is a kind and gentle soul, beloved by all who know her."

"That, my dear Watson, is the crux of the matter. We must delve deeper into Miss Davenport's life and relationships to uncover any potential motives for her disappearance. Perhaps there is a jilted suitor, or a jealous rival, who may have cause to wish her ill."

Watson frowned. "It did strike me as odd that Miss Davenport left so suddenly. Mrs King told us Dorothy had received a letter confirming she had won a holiday. And yet, instead of taking the time to prepare for such a break, it appears Dorothy left in quite a rush. Surely if one wins a stay at a cottage, one could choose when they wish to go."

Sherlock held up one finger. "Unless someone wanted Miss Davenport there at a certain time for some reason. Or, this is something else we need to consider, someone could have wanted Miss Davenport to leave London quickly and not return for two weeks, and somehow made that happen."

"Why would they want her out of London?" Watson asked.

"That is what we are going to find out," Sherlock replied. He stood and strode over to the window. "I do wish Mrs Hudson would hasten back. We can't proceed with the next part of our investigation until she does."

Dr Watson joined him at the window. "She'll be back in due course; she won't let us down. Holmes, should we book our tickets to Devon soon? We told Mrs Fairfax we would visit Dorothy there."

Holmes looked at Watson. "Let's hold on a little longer and gather more information. I'm not entirely convinced Miss Davenport is in Devon, yet." He turned his attention back to the streets below, muttering impatiently under his breath for Mrs Hudson to return.

# Chapter 4

Another hour passed by as Sherlock and Watson awaited the return of their landlady. Sherlock attempted to keep himself busy by learning a new melody on his violin, and Dr Watson began filling in the crossword in the newspaper. They kept looking towards the door, expecting to see the welcome face of Mrs Hudson.

At last, the familiar sound of her footsteps echoed up the stairs, and she entered the sitting room, a triumphant smile upon her face and the notebook clutched in her hand.

"Ah, Mrs Hudson!" Sherlock exclaimed, setting aside his violin and rising to greet her. "I trust your visit to the boarding house was fruitful?"

Mrs Hudson nodded, settling herself into a chair and opening her notebook. "It was, Mr Holmes. I have gathered quite a bit of information about the boarding house and its residents."

Watson placed the newspaper on the table. "Do tell us, Mrs Hudson. What did you discover?"

Mrs Hudson began to recount her findings, her voice filled with enthusiasm. "I managed to speak to some of the lodgers and they were all quite surprised by Miss Davenport's sudden holiday, as it seemed quite out of character for her. None of the women I talked to had seen the letter about the holiday."

Sherlock nodded, his brow furrowed in thought. "And what of Miss Davenport's room? Did you have the opportunity to examine it?"

"I did," Mrs Hudson replied, looking through her notebook. "It's a small attic room, with solid walls and only one door in and out. The room is quite charming and cosy, in my opinion. The walls are painted a soft shade of powder blue, with a delicate floral wallpaper bordering the ceiling. Quite lovely. There's a sturdy wooden bed frame against one wall, adorned with a handmade quilt in shades of lavender and cream. I've got a similar one in green."

Watson smiled, picturing the cosy space in his mind's eye. "It sounds like a pleasant retreat, Mrs Hudson."

Mrs Hudson nodded. "It is, Dr Watson. There's a bedside table, with an oil lamp and a small vase of wildflowers. Opposite the bed, there's a simple writing desk tucked beneath the dormer window, with a quill pen, an inkwell, and a stack of books. The books are a mix of novels and reference books. Some of the novels are recently published stories. I saw 'The Time Machine' by H.G. Wells and 'The Jungle Book' by Rudyard Kipling."

Watson nodded. "A well-read young woman, it seems."

Mrs Hudson continued, describing the personal touches that adorned the room. "There are sketches and water-colour paintings on the walls, mainly of London's parks and gardens. Lovely, they are. A framed photograph of her sister and family is on the windowsill. There is only one armchair in the room. It looked worn, but comfy."

Sherlock smiled. "Mrs Hudson, you have been most thorough in your findings. I am most impressed and think you may have picked up on more details than I would have."

Mrs Hudson chuckled. "Oh, I wouldn't say that, Mr Holmes. I just notice things like the wallpaper and furniture."

"And what of storage, Mrs Hudson? Did you note anything of interest?" Watson asked.

"There is a wardrobe in one corner and a small dresser in the other." She looked up from her notes, a rather stern look in her eyes. "If you are going to ask me if I looked in those items, then I am going to say no, I didn't. A woman's belongings deserve respect, no matter if she is in the room or not."

Feeling like he'd been chastised, Sherlock nodded and said gently, "I understand, but do we know if Miss Davenport took some clothes before she left?"

"She did," Mrs Hudson confirmed. "One woman I spoke to, Sally, helped Miss Davenport down the stairs with her packed suitcase a few days ago and she said it was heavy enough to contain sufficient clothes for a two-week holiday. I did have a quick look for the letter you mentioned, the one about the holiday, but I didn't find anything out in the open in Dorothy's bedroom. But according to Sally, Dorothy said the letter was firmly tucked in her handbag."

"I see," Sherlock replied. "Did you observe any evidence of a hasty departure? Anything out of place or suggesting that Miss Davenport left in a hurry?"

Mrs Hudson paused for a moment, her brow furrowed in thought as she mentally retraced her steps through the room. "No, Mr Holmes," she replied, shaking her head. "Everything seemed to be in its proper place. The bed was neatly made, and there were no signs of disarray or rushed packing."

"It seems that we are left with more questions than answers," Sherlock mused. "The lack of any sign of a hurried exit or proof of a holiday won suggests that there may be more to this case than meets the eye."

Mrs Hudson closed the notebook and said, "I must say, I rather enjoyed playing the role of detective for a while. It was quite thrilling to be a part of your investigation, even in a small way. I hope I have been of use."

Sherlock smiled. "Your assistance has been invaluable, Mrs Hudson," he said, his tone sincere. "Your keen observations and attention to detail have provided us with valuable insights into Miss Davenport's character and circumstances."

Mrs Hudson beamed with pride, her cheeks flushing slightly at the praise. "Well, I am always at your disposal, Mr Holmes," she said. "If you and Dr Watson ever require my help again, you need only ask."

Watson smiled. "I have no doubt that we shall call upon your services again, Mrs Hudson," he said, his voice laced with fondness. "Why don't you keep that notebook in case you need to use it again in a future investigation?"

Mrs Hudson held the notebook closer. "Thank you. I'll do that. Now, gentlemen, I will return to the kitchen and make a start on preparing dinner. I assume you will be in for the rest of the day."

"I'm afraid not," Sherlock answered as he rose to his feet. "We have another call to make before this day is over."

"We do?" Watson asked.

"We do, and we need to leave immediately," Sherlock replied.

"Rightio," Watson said, giving his half-finished crossword a wistful look. "I'll get my coat."

# Chapter 5

Holmes and Watson took a hansom cab to their next destination, the home of Lord and Lady Cavendish. Watson asked Holmes what information they hoped to discover there.

Sherlock answered, "I wonder if Miss Davenport's disappearance is connected to her role as a social secretary for Lord and Lady Cavendish."

"Ah, I see. It's a possibility, Holmes," Watson said. "Miss Davenport's position would have granted her access to the inner workings of the Cavendish household and their social circles. From what I have read in the papers, the social events organised by Lord and Lady Cavendish are lavish affairs with no expense spared. Are you suggesting that someone is now covering for Miss Davenport during her absence? Someone who intends to commit a crime? And could it be this person who orchestrated Miss Davenport's unexpected departure?"

Sherlock smiled at his friend. "It would be the perfect cover for someone with nefarious intentions, to infiltrate the Cavendish household, once they had taken Miss Davenport out of the picture, and carry out their plans undetected in their role as a temporary secretary."

Watson asked, "But who would have the means and motive to carry out such a scheme?"

Sherlock answered, "That is what we must discover. I hope someone is at home to receive us. We should have sent a telegram requesting a meeting with Lord and Lady Cavendish, but time is of the essence."

The hansom cab soon arrived at the grand residence of Lord and Lady Cavendish. The house, situated in one of London's most exclusive neighbourhoods, stood tall and proud. The immaculately manicured gardens and the gleaming brass fixtures on the front door spoke of luxury and refinement.

Sherlock knocked on the front door. It was opened by a well-dressed butler who gave them an enquiring look.

Sherlock bowed his head. "I sincerely apologise for our unannounced visit, but may we speak with Lord and Lady Cavendish, if they are at home? I am Sherlock Holmes, and this is Dr John Watson."

The butler said, "May I ask what this is in connection with?"

"It's a matter concerning Miss Dorothy Davenport."

At the mention of Dorothy's name, the butler's look softened. He opened the door wider and invited them in. He told them Lord Cavendish was at home and was sure he would talk with them.

The butler led them through the marble-floored foyer and into an impressive drawing room. The room was adorned with fine art, antique furniture, and plush velvet curtains that framed the large windows overlooking the meticulously landscaped gardens. The butler offered them refreshments, which they politely declined, before informing them that Lord Cavendish would be with them shortly.

As they waited, Sherlock looked around the room, taking in every detail, while Watson marvelled at the grandeur of their surroundings. The sound of footsteps approaching drew their attention, and they rose to greet Lord Cavendish as he entered the room.

"Mr Holmes, Dr Watson," Lord Cavendish said warmly, extending his hand in greeting. "What a pleasure to meet you. I must admit, I am rather surprised by your visit."

Sherlock shook the Lord's hand firmly. "Thank you for seeing us, Lord Cavendish. We are here on a matter of some urgency, regarding your social secretary, Miss Dorothy Davenport, and her sudden departure from London."

Lord Cavendish's brow furrowed slightly as he gestured for them to take a seat. "Yes, I was quite surprised when Miss Davenport informed me of her holiday plans at such short notice. She's always been such a dedicated and hard-working member of our staff, but I suppose even the most diligent among us needs a break from time to time." He settled into a plush armchair opposite them.

"The thing is, Lord Cavendish," Watson said, glancing at Sherlock before continuing. "Miss Davenport's sister, Mrs Agnes Fairfax, came to us with concerns about her sudden departure. She said it was quite out of character for Miss Davenport to take off so suddenly, and without informing her family beforehand of her intentions."

Lord Cavendish nodded thoughtfully. "I can understand Mrs Fairfax's concern, but I assure you, Miss Davenport was in good spirits when she informed me of her plans. She said she'd won a holiday in a competition and was looking forward to a rest before returning to work with renewed energy."

Sherlock said, "Lord Cavendish, has Miss Davenport's absence caused any disruption to your social calendar? I imagine her role is quite crucial in the planning and execution of your events."

Lord Cavendish shook his head. "Not at all, Mr Holmes," he said, a note of pride in his voice. "Miss Davenport is an exceptionally organised individual. Before her departure, she ensured that all of our upcoming events were meticulously planned and arranged. From the guest lists to the RSVPs and the catering, everything is in place and will run like clockwork, even in her absence."

Sherlock nodded. "I see. And have you appointed a temporary replacement for Miss Davenport?"

Lord Cavendish shook his head once more. "There was no need. Miss Davenport's planning is so thorough that we are more than capable of handling the events she has arranged without the need for additional staff."

"Lord Cavendish, if you would indulge me for a moment, I would like to know more about Miss Davenport as a person," Sherlock said. "What is she like, both in her professional capacity and on a more personal level?"

Lord Cavendish smiled warmly, his eyes reflecting a genuine fondness for his social secretary. "Miss Davenport is an exceptional individual, Mr Holmes. In her professional life, she is the epitome of efficiency and organisation. Her attention to detail is unparalleled, and she handles even the most complex social events with grace and poise." The nobleman paused for a moment as if collecting his thoughts, before continuing. "On a personal level, Miss Davenport is well-liked by all who have the pleasure of knowing her. She is unfailingly polite and courteous, treating everyone she encounters with the utmost respect, regardless of their station in life. Her kind and gentle nature has endeared her to many, both within our household and beyond."

Watson asked, "In your opinion, does Miss Davenport have any enemies? Anyone who might wish her harm or seek to disrupt her life in some way?"

Lord Cavendish shook his head firmly. "No, Dr Watson, I cannot imagine anyone harbouring ill will towards Miss Davenport. She is a true gem, and her presence brings nothing but joy and light to those around her. If she has any enemies, I am not aware of them."

Sherlock rose from his seat and extended his hand to Lord Cavendish. "Thank you for your time and insight. Your words have been most helpful in our investigation."

Lord Cavendish shook Sherlock's hand warmly, a smile on his face. "It is my pleasure, Mr Holmes. If there is anything else I can do to assist you, please do not hesitate to ask. In my opinion, Mrs Fairfax has no need to worry about her sister. I am certain Miss Davenport will return from her holiday rested and happy in due course."

With a final nod of thanks, Sherlock and Watson took their leave, stepping out into the bright sunlight of the London street.

"Watson," Sherlock said, "I believe it is time for us to journey to Devon. We must speak with Miss Davenport directly to clear up this confusion surrounding her holiday, if only to put her sister's mind at rest. Speaking of Mrs Fairfax, I must send her a telegram before we head to Devon, and let her know how our investigation is proceeding."

Watson looked back at the impressive home behind them. "Holmes, I have a strange feeling about Miss Davenport."

"Go on," Sherlock prompted.

Watson looked back at him. "What if we are looking at this case from the wrong angle? What if there wasn't a competition at all and Miss Davenport took herself to Devon for some reason?" Sherlock's smile increased. "My dear Watson, if I didn't know any better, I would wager you are a mind-reader. I was just pondering the same thing.

Yes, if Miss Davenport arranged her own sudden departure, it begs the question, why?"

"Indeed," Watson said. "Why would she need to be away from London at this time? Away from her lodgings, her family, and her place of work. Is she up to something? Or is she running away from something or someone?"

"All great questions, and ones we will find answers to." Sherlock hailed a cab." Watson, it's too late to get a train to Devon tonight, but let's make our way to the station and purchase tickets for the earliest departure tomorrow. I would like to speak to Miss Dorothy Davenport as soon as possible. Considering how long the journey will take us, we should find somewhere to stay overnight once we arrive in Devon."

Watson said, "And if we don't find Miss Davenport in Devon, what will we do then?"

Sherlock flashed him a smile. "Then, my dear friend, we will pursue a different avenue of investigation. I'm not sure what, but I'm certain something will come to us if the need arises."

# Chapter 6

Early the next morning, and with their overnight bags packed, Sherlock and Watson got ready to bid farewell to Mrs Hudson and set off on their journey to Devon.

Mrs Hudson insisted on packing some provisions for their journey in case Holmes and Watson didn't like the refreshments provided on the train. She said, "Best to be prepared, I always say," as she handed Dr Watson a small basket filled with carefully wrapped sandwiches, pastries and fruit in wax paper.

Sherlock smiled at their landlady. "Mrs Hudson, how would we ever manage without you? Your thoughtfulness and generosity fills my heart with gratitude."

Mrs Hudson waved his words away and told her tenants to take good care of themselves on their journey.

Holmes and Watson left their home and hurried along the streets towards King's Cross Station. When they arrived, the bustling terminal was alive with activity, as travellers from all walks of life hurried to and fro, their voices mingling in a cacophony of excitement and anticipation. The air was thick with the scent of coal smoke and the hissing of steam engines. The trains waited like resting dragons on the lines, curls of smoke drifting from their funnels.

Holmes and Watson boarded their train and located the first-class carriage they had booked the night before. Their luggage was stowed overhead.

A short while later, the whistle blew, and the train lurched forward.

Dr Watson settled back in his upholstered seat and sighed contentedly. "I love travelling on trains. There's something, oh, I don't know, something magical about them, don't you think, Holmes?"

Sherlock nodded. "There is. And this journey will give us time to discuss Miss Davenport's case and what questions we need to ask her. Should we find her, of course."

Dr Watson reached into his pocket and pulled out his notebook. He opened it and said, "I have already recorded my thoughts on the matter. It took me a while to get to sleep last night, so I decided to make use of my restless state."

"I am interested to hear your thoughts," Sherlock said leaning forward. "Please, proceed."

As the train pulled out of the station, Dr Watson and Holmes discussed the matter of Dorothy Davenport. They soon agreed to a course of action, and then the matter was put to one side.

Dr Watson opened out the newspaper he had bought on the way to the station, determined to finish that day's crossword.

Sherlock settled back more in his comfy seat and looked out of the window at the passing scenery of London, taking in its familiar sights. Before too long, the scenery changed and the countryside began to unfold before his eyes. Rolling hills, verdant fields, and picturesque villages dotted the landscape, their beauty enhanced by the golden hues of the rising sun.

The rhythmic chugging of the engine filled the air as the train took them further away from London.

The journey was a long one; the train winding its way through the picturesque countryside of England. The two men kept themselves occupied with a variety of things to pass the time. Watson, having completed the crossword, perused the rest of the newspaper, occasionally reading aloud an article of interest, while Sherlock alternated between gazing pensively out of the window and jotting down notes in his notebook. They engaged in lively discussions, their conversation ranging from the particulars of the case to the latest advancements in science and medicine. The miles slipped away beneath the rhythmic clacking of the train's wheels, bringing them ever closer to their destination and the mystery that awaited them in the village of Clovelly.

Much to Sherlock's annoyance, there were several delays along the way and their journey took far longer than they had anticipated. When the train finally pulled into the town nearest to Clovelly, night had well and truly fallen. The platform was dimly lit by flickering gas lamps, casting eerie shadows across the weathered brickwork.

Sherlock and Watson disembarked, their bags in hand, and made their way to the station exit. There, they found a friendly local man with a horse and cart. Sherlock asked if there was a nearby inn where they could spend the night.

The friendly chap said he knew just the place and invited Holmes and Watson to take a seat in his cart.

The cart wound its way through the streets of the town, the full moon shining brightly above them.

Soon, they arrived at the inn, a warm and inviting establishment with a cheerful fire crackling in the hearth. The innkeeper, a jovial man with rosy cheeks and a twinkle in his eyes, greeted them warmly and showed them to their rooms.

After a hearty dinner of local fare, Sherlock and Watson retired to their respective chambers, ready to locate the elusive Miss Davenport the following day.

# Chapter 7

The next morning, after a hearty breakfast at the inn, Sherlock and Watson arranged for a horse-drawn carriage to take them to the cottage where Dorothy Davenport was staying in Clovelly.

As they travelled along the winding country roads, Sherlock and Watson marvelled at the stunning scenery. Rolling hills, lush green fields, and charming cottages dotted the landscape, each one more picturesque than the last.

Finally, the carriage arrived at a charming cottage with roses growing around the door. The scent of the blooms was intoxicating, and the sight of the sea in the distance was breathtaking. Holmes asked the driver if he could wait for them, as he wasn't sure how long their visit would take. The driver was happy to do so and leaned back in his seat, enjoying the warmth of the morning sunshine.

Sherlock and Watson walked towards the cottage. They noticed a young woman in the front garden. She was resting on a wooden chair next to a table. She seemed lost in thought, her gaze fixed on the distant horizon.

"Miss Davenport, I presume?" Sherlock called out, his voice carrying across the garden.

The woman turned, startled by the sudden interruption. "Yes, that's me," she replied, rising from her chair. "And who might you be?"

Sherlock and Watson introduced themselves, explaining the purpose of their visit. "Your sister, Mrs Agnes Fairfax, has engaged our services," Sherlock explained. "She is quite concerned about your sudden departure and asked us to look into the matter."

Dorothy sighed, a rueful smile on her face. "I'm not at all surprised," she said, gesturing for the two men to join her at the table. "Agnes has always been a worrier, and I know my sudden trip must have seemed quite out of character. I normally plan such events months in advance, sometimes years. So, yes, I can understand why she engaged your services. Although, I fear you may have had a wasted journey. But seeing as you're here now, would you like a cup of tea? There's plenty in the pot."

Holmes and Watson took their seats at the table, and Dorothy poured them each a cup of steaming tea. The aroma of the freshly brewed beverage mingled with the sweet scent of the roses, creating a delightful ambience in the cottage garden.

"Now, Miss Davenport," Sherlock began, his keen eyes studying her expression, "would you be so kind as to tell us more about this prize you've won?"

Dorothy smiled, a hint of confusion in her hazel eyes. "To be perfectly honest, Mr Holmes, I was rather surprised to receive the news myself. I couldn't recall entering any competitions recently, but then I wondered if it might have been part of a charity event I'd organised for Lord and Lady Cavendish. I do make small donations from time to time, you see, and I have bought raffle tickets on some occasions, but I never check to see if I've won anything. I always assumed I'd be notified if I had won anything. When the letter arrived confirming I'd won a holiday here, I automatically presumed it was something connected with my work."

Watson took a sip of his tea and then said, "And did you confirm the legitimacy of the prize?"

"Oh, yes," Dorothy replied. "The letter had come straight from the owners of this cottage. I contacted them by telegram to confirm the details and was told that the person who had rented the cottage as a prize wished to remain anonymous. One thing did puzzle me, though. The letter said I was to claim my prize immediately or else I would lose the holiday. Which seemed strange to me. Surely, if you win a holiday, you should be free to choose when to take that holiday, within reason, of course."

"Yes!" Dr Watson exclaimed. "That's exactly what I said to Holmes."

Dorothy continued, "Bearing the restricted date in mind, I had to take my leave more abruptly than I wished to. Fortunately, Lord and Lady Cavendish were agreeable to my unexpected leave, and I made sure everything was in place for all upcoming social events. But even so, a worrying thought niggled me about the time restriction placed upon my prize. Even though I had received a reassuring telegram from the cottage owners, I had to take my safety into account."

"Of course," Dr Watson said. "A most sensible attitude considering you didn't know the identity of the person who is behind this prize."

Dorothy nodded in agreement. "Luckily, I have a friend who lives in Clovelly, Mary. We grew up as neighbours in Birmingham, and when she moved away, we kept in touch. Mary moved to Clovelly a few years ago with her new husband. Her letters were full of the beauty and the charm of this place. She extended an open invitation to me and said I could stay with her and her husband whenever I felt the need to escape London. So, when I received the letter about the holiday, I contacted Mary and told her about it. She thought it was a most peculiar situation, but said it was the perfect opportunity for me to finally visit her. And, if the cottage holiday was a jape of some kind, then at least I would have somewhere safe to stay when I arrived."

Dr Watson said, "And did you contact Mary upon your arrival in Clovelly?"

Dorothy laughed. "She was waiting for me when I arrived by horse and cart, her husband at her side. They insisted on staying with me for a few hours in this cottage to make sure everything was above board. The key was where the cottage owners said it would be, and the owners had kindly provided food and drinks for me. Once Mary was satisfied the cottage was a safe place for me to stay, we paid a visit to the cottage owners, who live a few streets away. They showed me the correspondence they had received from the anonymous person behind the prize. Again, everything seemed above board, albeit of a secretive nature."

Sherlock asked, "In what form was the correspondence between this anonymous person and the cottage owner?"

"It was all by telegrams," Dorothy explained. "The ones coming from the unknown person were sent from a central London office."

Sherlock said, "And you are satisfied everything is in order, in the legal sense?"

"Oh, yes, I am. And so is Mary." Dorothy glanced towards the sea. "I am enjoying the respite. It's been quite lovely to take a break from the hustle and bustle of London. If I ever find out who organised this holiday, I shall thank them most sincerely."

"Miss Davenport," Sherlock began, "have you considered the possibility that there might be something more sinister at play here? That perhaps someone wanted you out of the way for a specific reason?"

Dorothy's eyes widened, a flicker of unease passing over her delicate features. "Sinister? I... I hadn't really thought about it like that. What do you mean, Mr Holmes?"

Sherlock explained, "Well, let us consider the facts. You are a woman of routine, Miss Davenport, not prone to sudden, unplanned trips. And yet, here you are, the recipient of a mysterious prize that whisked you away from London at a moment's notice. It's all rather convenient, wouldn't you say?"

Watson nodded, setting down his teacup. "I agree. Miss Davenport, is there anyone at your boarding house or in your work with Lord and Lady Cavendish who might have cause to want you out of the way, and at this particular time?"

Dorothy frowned. "I can't imagine why anyone would want me gone, Dr Watson."

Sherlock said, "And yet, the timing of this surprise holiday is most curious. It's possible that someone saw an opportunity to remove you from the equation, for reasons that remain, as yet, unclear."

Dorothy's face paled. "But who would do such a thing? And why? I can't believe that anyone would go to such lengths to get rid of me."

Watson placed a reassuring hand on Dorothy's arm. "We don't know for certain that there is anything dubious at play here, Miss Davenport. But it is our job to investigate all avenues."

Sherlock nodded, his expression grave. "And that is precisely what we intend to do. It might be wise for you to return to London with us. It concerns me that the person who rented this cottage wished to remain anonymous. Or, if you wish to continue with your holiday, perhaps you could stay with your friend until we find out who is behind this gift of yours. Your safety is paramount."

Dorothy said, "Given your concerns, I will stay with Mary. But please, keep me informed of any developments, Mr Holmes. I need to know what's going on."

"You have my word, Miss Davenport," Sherlock replied, rising from his chair. "We will return to London and continue with our investigations there. We will get to the truth of this matter, no matter where it leads us. In the meantime, try to enjoy your stay in this charming village. We will be in touch. Before we go, is there anything else you wish to tell us? Have you any social events coming up that you will now miss because of your stay here?"

Dorothy considered the question. "The only event I'm missing is my book club. The meeting is booked for this Friday evening at six p.m. We meet every month."

Sherlock paused. "Tell me more about this book club, Miss Davenport. Where is it held, and who attends?"

Dorothy's face lit up as she spoke. She told Sherlock about the book club, where it was held, and the three other women who attend it.

Dr Watson recorded the information in his notebook.

She said, "It's not just a place to discuss our love of reading, it's always a place to talk about our personal lives, too."

"Such as?" Sherlock asked.

"Oh, you know, the usual things," Dorothy explained. "I talk about my family and how quickly my nephews are growing. Sometimes, I talk about the events I had organised and the people who attended them."

"I see," Sherlock said. "And had you also spoken about your friend, Mary, who lives here?"

Dorothy laughed. "Yes, I often talked about her and how I would love to take a holiday here."

Sherlock looked closer at Miss Davenport. "May I ask, did you talk about any upcoming events that you have organised for Lord and Lady Cavendish?"

Dorothy's cheeks coloured. "Well, yes, even though I know I shouldn't. I only mentioned the briefest of details, though, such as where and when the event would be held." She frowned. "Is this important, Mr Holmes?"

"It could be," Sherlock answered. "Thank you for your time, Miss Davenport. We'll be sure to keep you informed of any developments in our investigation. I will send a telegram to your sister to confirm we have seen you in good health."

"Thank you," Dorothy said.

As they bid farewell to Dorothy and made their way back to the waiting horse and carriage, Sherlock turned to Watson with a determined expression. "We must return to London immediately, Watson. I have a feeling that Miss Davenport's book club may hold the key to this mystery."

Watson nodded. "Do you suspect one of the members might be involved in her sudden holiday?"

"It's too early to say for certain," Sherlock replied. "But I do feel one of them could be behind Miss Davenport's hasty holiday."

# Chapter 8

The following day, after an exhausted sleep following their long return journey from Devon, Holmes suggested to Watson that they call upon the members of Miss Davenport's book club, starting with Miss Lillian Goodwin.

Watson nodded, setting down his morning cup of tea. "Agreed, Holmes. Perhaps she can shed some light on any tensions or rivalries within the group that might have led to Miss Davenport's removal."

With their plan set, the two men finished their breakfast and set out for the Goodwin residence, a grand townhouse located in one of London's more affluent neighbourhoods. Upon their arrival, they were greeted by a stern-faced butler, who ushered them into a well-appointed drawing room to await Miss Goodwin.

Lillian Goodwin swept into the room a few moments later, her elegant gown rustling as she moved. She regarded

Holmes and Watson with a curious expression, her eyebrows raised in surprise.

"Mr Holmes, Dr Watson," she said, extending her hand in greeting. "To what do I owe the pleasure of this unexpected visit?"

Holmes bowed slightly. "We apologise for the intrusion, Miss Goodwin, but we are here on a matter of some urgency. It concerns your friend and fellow book club member, Miss Dorothy Davenport."

Lillian's eyes widened, a flicker of something unreadable crossing her features before she composed herself. "Dorothy? Is she all right? Has something happened?"

Watson stepped forward, his voice gentle. "Miss Davenport has won a holiday to Devon, quite unexpectedly. She left without informing her sister, who was extremely worried about her sudden departure, and asked Mr Holmes and myself to look into the matter. We were hoping you might have some insight into the situation."

Lillian's lips curved into a smile that didn't quite reach her eyes. "A holiday? How lovely for her. I had no idea she had left town. I suppose that means she won't be at our book club this Friday. What a shame."

Holmes' gaze intensified. "And yet, you don't seem entirely surprised by this development, Miss Goodwin.

Might there be some tension within your book club that could have led to Miss Davenport's sudden absence?"

Lillian's smile faltered, her fingers twisting the fabric of her gown. "Tension? No, of course not. We're all the best of friends in the book club. It's true that Dorothy and I don't always see eye to eye on the books we read, but that's hardly cause for concern."

Watson's brow furrowed. "Could you elaborate on that, Miss Goodwin? What sort of disagreements have you had with Miss Davenport?"

Lillian sighed, a hint of exasperation creeping into her voice. "Oh, it's nothing serious, really. Dorothy has a tendency to dismiss the romance novels that I suggest as reading material for the group. She looks down on them and claims the novels are 'unrealistic nonsense.' She prefers those dreadful adventure stories, always going on about how they're more intellectually stimulating. It can be quite grating at times."

Holmes said, "And with Miss Davenport gone, I suppose you'll be free to choose the next book for your club without opposition?"

Lillian's eyes flashed with something akin to triumph. "As a matter of fact, yes. I already have the perfect novel in mind, a delightful romance set in the Italian countryside.

I'm sure the other ladies will be thrilled to read something a bit lighter for a change. I love reading romances. I always have. They inspire me to look for the romance in my life. I hope one day to find my one true love; someone who will make me his beloved wife. That special man who I'll spend the rest of my days with." She glanced wistfully towards the window as if expecting to see her knight in shining armour standing there with love shining in his eyes just for her.

Watson's expression grew serious. "Miss Goodwin, I must ask. Did you have anything to do with Miss Davenport's sudden holiday? Perhaps as a way to ensure your book choice would prevail?"

Lillian's face flushed with indignation. "Certainly not, Dr Watson! I may not always agree with Dorothy's taste in literature, but I would never stoop so low as to orchestrate her removal from the book club. The very idea is absurd!"

Dr Watson said, "I apologise. I did not mean to upset you, but we have certain questions that we need to ask."

Lillian gave him a stern look and said coldly, "Are there any other 'certain' questions you need to ask? I have a busy day ahead of me, and many social engagements to attend."

Holmes said, "One more question, if I may. How do you get on with the other members in the book group? Miss Harris and Miss Brown?"

"Like I told you mere minutes ago, Mr Holmes, we are the best of friends." Lillian ran her hands smoothly down her silk gown. "Is there anything else?"

Sherlock said, "We have no further questions, Miss Goodwin. We appreciate your time and candour. If you think of anything else that might be relevant to our investigation, please don't hesitate to contact us."

As they took their leave from the building, Watson said to Holmes. "Do you believe her? Could Miss Goodwin have had a hand in Miss Davenport's disappearance? I imagine Lillian is receiving a wealthy allowance, which would give her the funds to rent that cottage in Clovelly."

Holmes shook his head, his eyes distant. "I'm not certain, Watson. But one thing is clear – there is more to this book club than meets the eye. Let's call on Miss Esther Harris next and see what she has to say."

# Chapter 9

Holmes and Watson stepped into the bustling office where Esther Harris worked as a bookkeeper in her father's accountancy firm. After speaking to Esther's father and giving him the reason for their visit, Holmes and Watson were shown to Miss Harris' desk.

"Esther," Mr Harris said as they approached the young woman. "You have some visitors. Mr Holmes and Dr Watson. Don't be alarmed. They merely wish to talk to you about Dorothy."

Esther's eyes widened in alarm. "Dorothy? Is she okay?"

"Perfectly fine," Holmes answered, smiling at Miss Harris. "As your father said, we have a few questions for you, if we may take up some of your time?"

Mr Harris pointed towards a meeting room and suggested they talk in there. Holmes thanked him and then followed Esther as she led the way.

Esther took her visitors into the room and closed the door behind them.

She said, "Please, have a seat. What would you like to know about Dorothy?" She sat opposite them, concern in her eyes.

Holmes explained about Dorothy's sudden departure from London because of the holiday she had apparently won.

Esther shook her head. "I can't take it in. Taking off like that is certainly out of character for Dorothy. She never does anything on the spur of the moment. Where has she gone on this holiday?"

Sherlock replied, "Clovelly in Devon."

Esther smiled. "Ah, now I understand. Dorothy often talks about going to Clovelly for a break. She has a friend who lives there who is always telling her how lovely it is. I suppose that if Dorothy had the chance to go there, she would have made all the arrangements in double-quick time. She's organised enough to do so. Good for her. I hope she's having a relaxing time."

Holmes asked, "And what is your relationship with Miss Davenport, if I may ask?"

Esther said, "Dorothy and I have been friends for years. We set up the book club together about a year ago. She's always been so kind and supportive, even when we disagree on the books we read."

Watson raised an eyebrow. "Disagree? How so?"

Esther chuckled. "Oh, you know how it is with book clubs. Everyone has their own tastes and preferences. Dorothy tends to favour adventure stories, while I lean more towards historical fiction. But we've always managed to find common ground and we respect each other's opinions."

Holmes nodded. "And what of the other members of your book club? Do you know them well?"

Esther's smile faltered slightly. "I know Lillian, of course. She's been a member for as long as I have. And then there's Violet Brown, but I'm afraid I don't know her very well. She's a recent addition to the group."

"Miss Violet Brown?" Dr Watson said. "We were hoping to speak with her, but Miss Davenport couldn't provide us with her address. Do you happen to know where she lives?"

Esther replied, "I'm afraid I don't. Violet only joined our book club about four months ago. She met Dorothy at a charity event where Violet was working as a waitress."

Dr Watson asked, "And how did Miss Brown become a member of your club?"

"Well, according to Violet, she and Dorothy got chatting at the end of the event, and the book club came up in conversation. Violet mentioned she was a keen reader, so Dorothy invited her to the group."

Watson frowned. "That seems rather generous of Miss Davenport, to invite a stranger to join your group."

Esther nodded. "That's what I thought, too. In fact, Dorothy later confided in me that she couldn't really remember talking to Violet at all, or even meeting her. But Dorothy felt it would be rude to ask her to leave the group as Violet had already been to one meeting and seemed to get along with everyone."

Holmes asked Esther, "And what do you make of Miss Violet Brown?"

Esther hesitated, her fingers fidgeting with the edge of her sleeve. "To be honest, there's something about her that doesn't quite ring true. At the second book club meeting, she told us she no longer works as a waitress, but now works as a governess, but she's been very vague about the family she works for and where they live. It seemed a strange progression to me; to be a waitress one month, and then a governess the next. And it's not just that, it's just a feeling I get, like she's not being her true self."

Holmes smiled. "Intuition can be a powerful tool, Miss Harris. Often, our subconscious picks up on subtle cues that our conscious mind might miss."

Esther said, "I suppose so. I think Dorothy might have felt the same way, even though she didn't share her feelings with me. At the meetings, after we had talked about the book, we would chat about our everyday lives. Violet would always ask Dorothy lots of questions about her work. You know, like when and where was the next social event being held? Who would be there? That sort of thing. I could see how uncomfortable Dorothy felt about Violet's constant questioning. Dorothy had talked about her work before Violet was a member of the group, as had I, but we never went into much detail, not as much detail as Violet was demanding of Dorothy of late."

"Did Violet show the same level of interest in your work?" Sherlock asked.

Esther smiled. "Not at all. She didn't show any interest in Lillian's life either. It was almost as if we were insignificant to her. She was only interested in Dorothy, or rather, Dorothy's work."

"That is very useful information, Miss Harris," Sherlock said. "Thank you for sharing that with us. Is there anything else you wish us to know about the book club, or Violet Brown?"

Esther shook her head. "Not that I can think of. Mr Holmes, do you think Dorothy took that sudden holiday to get away from Violet? Maybe Dorothy made up the excuse about winning it in a competition because she was becoming frightened of Violet somehow."

Sherlock frowned. "Ah, now that's something I haven't considered yet. That's an interesting observation, Miss Harris. I am beginning to think that Miss Violet Brown has got something to do with Dorothy leaving London, although the reasoning behind that is not clear to me."

"Yet," Esther added confidently. "I know you'll find out what's going on, Mr Holmes. My father always says there will never be a mystery that you and Dr Watson can't solve. And I agree." She smiled from one man to the other.

"Thank you," Holmes replied with a smile. "Your confidence in our abilities is pleasing to hear."

With that, Holmes and Watson took their leave, ready to take the next step in their investigation, and hopefully, one step closer to solving it.

# Chapter 10

Holmes and Watson headed to the building where the book club meetings were held. It was a modern four-storey townhouse, part of a row of buildings that included both businesses and shops. As they entered the reception area, they were greeted by a helpful man behind the desk.

"Good afternoon, gentlemen," the receptionist said with a friendly smile. "How may I assist you today?"

Holmes said, "We're here to inquire about the book club that meets in this building. I believe a Miss Dorothy Davenport is a member?"

The receptionist nodded, his expression turning thoughtful. "Ah, yes, Miss Davenport's book club. They meet here every month, always in the same room."

Sherlock asked, "And which room would that be?"

"It's the one at the very top of the building," the receptionist replied. "Miss Davenport has been booking it for their meetings for quite a while now. In fact, she's already reserved it monthly for the rest of this year."

Holmes nodded. "I see. And is that room used for any other purposes?"

The receptionist shook his head. "No, sir. It's mainly a storage area, but the book club ladies are the only ones who use it regularly. Apparently, it's in a convenient location for all of them, given where their homes are."

"Interesting," Holmes mused. "Would it be possible for us to take a look at the room?"

The receptionist hesitated for a moment, then nodded. "I don't see why not."

Holmes and Watson climbed the stairs to the top floor, their footsteps echoing in the narrow stairwell. When they reached the landing, they faced a plain wooden door with a simple brass handle.

Holmes tried the handle, and the door swung open easily. The room beyond was of medium size and dimly lit, with a few dusty bookcases standing flush against the walls and a scattering of mismatched chairs arranged around a low table.

Watson moved to one of the bookshelves, running his finger along the spines of the books. "These don't look like they've been touched in years," he remarked.

Holmes nodded, his glance sweeping the room. "Yes. It seems this room is used for little else besides the book club meetings. Despite the shabbiness of the room, it offers a cosy feel and I can imagine the ladies speaking freely about their chosen books here, and also, their personal lives."

Holmes moved to the window, peering out at the street below. The view was unremarkable, just a narrow alleyway and the backs of the neighbouring buildings.

He turned to face Watson. "Let's say that someone in the book club wanted Miss Davenport out of the picture before their next meeting, which takes place this Friday. But why would one of them want Dorothy out of the way?"

Watson said, "Miss Lillian Goodwin has made it clear that she clashes with Dorothy over their book choices. And with Dorothy away, Miss Goodwin will now get to put her choice forward this month. But is that really a reason for this holiday win charade?"

"As you said earlier, Miss Goodwin likely has the funds to undertake such a project, and maybe she did it out of spite. Now, let's turn our thoughts to Esther Harris. I can't see any reason why she would want Dorothy out of the way. And yet, she was very keen to cast suspicions upon Violet Brown; a woman we have not met. Why is that?

Is Esther planning something that she will later blame on Violet? She has already sown the seeds of doubt about Miss Brown's character in our minds."

Watson sighed. "It's a lot to take in, Holmes. How do we proceed now?"

Holmes turned around slowly. "The answer lies in this room. Once we find out why it is so important, then we will discover who is behind this mystery. Watson, we must search this room thoroughly. Move every piece of furniture. Look under tables, behind paintings, lift the rugs. I am certain that will find something of great interest here."

"Rightio." Watson took off his jacket, not wanting to get dust on it. "I'll take this side of the room, if that's okay with you."

Holmes nodded.

The duo started their search of the room, leaving no rug unturned and no bookcase unmoved.

It was Watson who found what they were looking for. He called Holmes over and pointed to an area behind one of the bookcases he had moved.

Sherlock rushed over. He broke into a wide smile when he saw what his friend had discovered. "Well done, Watson! This is exactly what I suspected might be in this room.

Now, we need to explore this area a little further. Are you ready?"

"Always," Watson said with a smile.

# Chapter 11

Late afternoon, three days later, Holmes and Watson returned to the street where the book club meeting was held, but instead of entering that building, they made their way to the adjacent structure, which housed an arts space. As they stepped inside, they were greeted by the sight of Lord Cavendish, who looked extremely worried.

Lord Cavendish approached Holmes and Watson, his face etched with worry. "Mr Holmes, please explain why you wished to meet me here. Your message was very vague. Has this got something to do with the charity event I'm holding here tonight?"

Sherlock said, "I believe it's got everything to do with your charity event, Lord Cavendish. I fear someone will attempt to steal the valuable artwork that will be displayed later on."

"But that's not possible," Lord Cavendish said. "We always have the highest security in place at such events. I can't imagine someone walking in off the street and stealing something."

Sherlock said, "Lord Cavendish, when will the artwork for the event arrive?"

The Lord checked his pocket watch. "Within the next hour. Usually, Miss Davenport would be here to ensure everything runs smoothly, but in light of her absence, I will be the one doing that. Not that there's much work involved, as Miss Davenport has given me a plan of where each piece will go."

Sherlock nodded. "And once the artwork is in place, will you leave the building?"

"I will," Lord Cavendish answered. "The event doesn't begin until eight p.m. I will return shortly before that to receive my guests, and my good wife will be with me."

"So, there will be a few hours where this building will be empty, and that will take place after the artwork has been put in place. Am I right?" Sherlock asked.

"Yes, that's right. I say, you don't think someone will try to break in during those hours, do you? This is a busy street, Mr Holmes, people will notice if someone is trying to get in. Surely."

Sherlock held up a finger. "Ah, they won't be breaking in from outside, Lord Cavendish. They will enter the building from an upstairs room. Please, let me explain. The building next door is where Miss Davenport and her friends hold their monthly book club meetings. They use the top room. A few days ago, Watson and I examined that room, and after moving one of the bookcases out of the way, we discovered a door which leads directly to the top room of this building. The door had been locked, but someone had recently forced the lock, making it easy to enter the room above.

"Watson and I went through that door and into this building. For a while, we couldn't work out why someone would want access to it. Then I remembered the events Miss Davenport organises for you. After making some enquiries, we found out about the event taking place tonight. Am I right in assuming the items on display will be valuable?"

Lord Cavendish nodded, his face pale. "Extremely valuable. We are hoping to raise a lot of money from them. But if they were to be stolen whilst in my care, my reputation would be ruined. Mr Holmes, has this proposed theft got something to do with Miss Davenport's sudden holiday?"

"It most certainly has," Sherlock replied. "Someone has come up with a devious plan, a very devious plan indeed. One of the ladies in the book club is behind this. Miss

Davenport must have told them about this event coming up, quite innocently, I believe, and I suspect she spoke about how precious the artwork is. That person wanted Dorothy out of the way, so that she wouldn't be at the book club meeting this month, which is taking place in a few hours. The person in question will use the adjoining door in the top room and will enter this building to commit the theft. She arranged for Miss Davenport to take a sudden holiday away from London, to a place Dorothy had often spoken about visiting, which made the alleged win even more attractive to her."

Lord Cavendish exclaimed, "Good grief! I can't believe someone would have the nerve to commit such a crime! Mr Holmes, do you know the identity of this woman? The one who is planning the theft?"

"I had my suspicions, and they were confirmed when I received some news earlier about Miss Lillian Goodwin and Miss Esther Harris, two members of the book club. Unfortunately, both women had been taken ill earlier today. It seems they were poisoned by chocolates that were delivered to their homes this morning. Thankfully, they received medical assistance and are now on the road to recovery." He shook his head. "I am annoyed with myself for not warning the ladies that something like this might happen. I have let them down most badly."

Watson spoke up, "Holmes, you weren't to know. You mustn't judge yourself too harshly."

"But I do, Watson. Things could have turned out much worse." Holmes sighed before continuing, "The person behind this devious plan is Miss Violet Brown. Well, that is the name she has given to the others. Violet first saw Miss Davenport at a charity event where Violet was working as a waitress. She realised Dorothy had access to people of wealthy means. Violet ingratiated herself into the book club and proceeded to bombard Dorothy with questions about upcoming events, hoping to pick the perfect one to commit a robbery. This event must have caught her attention, and Violet began to put her plan into place, starting with getting Dorothy out of the way."

"But why send her on holiday? That seems extreme," Lord Cavendish said.

"That's what I thought," Sherlock answered. "But maybe Dorothy was already becoming suspicious about Violet's endless questions and was about to voice her concerns to the others. Perhaps she was about to ask Violet to leave the group. That would ruin Violet's plans and it's possible she panicked and arranged the win to get Dorothy away as soon as possible."

Lord Cavendish nodded slowly, trying to take it all in. "And you assume this Miss Brown broke the lock on that door upstairs so that she could get into this building when the time was right?"

"I do," Sherlock confirmed. "Perhaps her first plan was to steal the keys to this place from Dorothy and enter through the front door as though she worked here. But after our examination of the room the other day, I spoke to the man on reception about the members of the book club. He said Miss Violet Brown was always the last one to leave, only by a few minutes, but that would have given her enough time to scope out the room to see if there was access anywhere. She must have been delighted to discover the door behind the bookcase. It has made her planned theft a lot easier."

Lord Cavendish shook his head in disbelief. "And you really think a theft will take place today?"

"All the evidence points to that," Sherlock said.

"So, what should I do? Cancel the event?"

"No, don't do that. The event should go ahead as planned. The thief needs to be caught in the act. We have to let Miss Brown proceed with her plan, and when she has the stolen items in her possession, an arrest can be made. She might not be working on her own, of course. She might turn up with extra people tonight. Perhaps she plans to tell the man on reception they are new members of the book club so as not to arouse suspicion."

"Seems she's thought of everything," Lord Cavendish mumbled, his brow furrowed in thought.

Sherlock said, "I have already contacted the police about this matter, and a small group of officers will be in attendance with Dr Watson and myself this afternoon. We will conceal ourselves behind some of the furniture in the upstairs room, and await Miss Brown's appearance. We will let her commit the theft, and the officers will arrest her as she returns to the room."

Lord Cavendish didn't look entirely convinced. "Mr Holmes, I respect your opinion, but it seems so very hard to believe. Is there any chance you could be wrong?"

Dr Watson took a sharp intake of breath.

Sherlock Holmes lifted his chin a fraction. "Lord Cavendish, I can assure you that I am not wrong. A theft will take place today."

# Chapter 12

Once the artwork had been delivered and put in place, and Lord Cavendish had left the building, Holmes, Watson, and a small contingent of police officers including Inspector Lestrade, concealed themselves behind an array of stored furniture in the top room. They kept silent as they waited for the thieves to make their move. The room was dimly lit, the shadows cast by the furniture providing ample cover for the waiting party.

Time seemed to crawl by, each second feeling like an eternity. Watson shifted uncomfortably, his leg cramping from the prolonged crouching position. Holmes, on the other hand, remained perfectly still, his keen eyes fixed on the door that connected the room to the upstairs chamber where the book club meetings took place.

Sometime later, the silence that had settled over the room was abruptly shattered by the grating sound of hinges as the door gradually swung open, the shadows of three figures spreading across the floor.  Low voices, barely above a whisper, drifted into the room, carrying with them an air of smug superiority. One voice, unmistakably feminine, stood out from the others, her words dripping with disdain and contempt.

"Can you believe these wealthy toffs?" the woman scoffed, her tone laced with a mixture of amusement and derision. "They've got nothing better to do than spend their hard-earned money on fancy artwork. Well, I'm more than happy to take it off their hands and put it to better use."

The woman's words were met with a chorus of harsh, grating laughter from her two male companions, their voices echoing in the confined space of the room.

"Too right, Violet," one of the men said. "They won't even know what hit 'em until it's far too late."

"We'll be long gone before they even realise their precious paintings are missing," the other man added. "By the time they discover the theft, we'll be halfway across the city, enjoying the fruits of our labour. And we'll make enough to pay for that holiday you organised. I don't know why you had to splash out like that, Vi."

The woman tutted. "I had to get her out of the way and away from the others. I could tell she was getting ready to kick me out of the club." She sniggered. "I wish I could see her face when she finds out about this theft. She'll know it's all her fault for going on and on about all the posh people she works for, and how much money they have. Serves her right."

The trio moved further into the room, their footsteps echoing on the hardwood floor. They were completely oblivious to the presence of Holmes, Watson, and the police officers hidden behind the furniture.

As the thieves made their way out of the room and down the stairs, Holmes signalled to the waiting officers to remain in position, his hand raised in a silent command. They needed to catch the culprits red-handed, with the stolen artwork in their possession, to ensure that justice would be served.

It wasn't long before the thieves returned, their voices once again filling the room, the sound of their self-congratulatory chatter shattering the tense silence.

"That was almost too easy," Violet crowed, her tone dripping with self-satisfaction.

"We'll be set for life with this haul," one of the men said. "No more scraping by, no more living hand to mouth. This is our ticket to the good life, and we've earned every penny of it."

At that very moment, Inspector Lestrade and his officers emerged from their carefully chosen hiding places.

"Police!" Lestrade shouted, his authoritative voice ringing out through the air, echoing off the walls of the gallery. "Drop the bags and put your hands in the air, now!"

The thieves froze instantly, their eyes growing wide with fear as they realised they had been caught completely off guard, the stolen artwork still clutched tightly in their trembling hands.

As the police officers moved in swiftly to apprehend the criminals, Holmes and Watson stepped forward.

Holmes fixed his piercing gaze on the woman, his voice calm and measured. "Miss Violet Brown, I presume?" he asked, his tone almost conversational, as if he were greeting an old acquaintance.

Violet's eyes narrowed, her lips curling into a sneer as she regarded the famous detective with undisguised contempt. "Sherlock Holmes," she spat, her voice dripping with venom, each word laced with a bitter hatred. "I should have known you'd stick your nose into this. Why can't you leave people like us alone? I should have sent you on holiday, too, got you out of the way. I'll know for next time."

"Next time?" Sherlock raised one eyebrow. "Are you sure there will be a next time?"

Violet Brown's only reply was a smug smile.

As the police officers handcuffed the thieves and led them away, Watson said to Holmes, "Another case solved, old friend," he said joyfully, clapping Holmes on the shoulder.

# Chapter 13

A week had passed since the dramatic events at the art gallery, and the city was still abuzz with talk of the foiled heist and the brilliant detective work of Sherlock Holmes and Dr John Watson. The newspapers had been filled with accounts of the daring arrest, each article more sensational than the last, and the public's fascination with the case showed no signs of abating.

On a crisp, sunny morning, Mrs Hudson ushered two visitors into the cosy confines of 221B Baker Street. Dorothy Davenport and her sister, Mrs Agnes Fairfax, were shown into the sitting room, where Holmes and Watson were enjoying a leisurely breakfast, the remnants of toast and marmalade scattered across the table. They stood as the women entered.

"Mr Holmes, Dr Watson," Dorothy began. "We simply had to come and express our gratitude in person. Your actions in apprehending Violet Brown and her accomplices were nothing short of heroic."

Mrs Fairfax nodded in agreement, her eyes shining with admiration. "We cannot thank you enough for your tireless efforts on our behalf. When I first came to you with my concerns about Dorothy's sudden disappearance, I never imagined it would lead to those criminals being arrested."

Holmes waved away their praise with a dismissive gesture. "Think nothing of it, ladies," he said, his voice warm and reassuring. "It is our duty and our pleasure to see justice served."

Dorothy lowered her gaze, her cheeks flushing with embarrassment. "I must admit, Mr Holmes, I feel terribly ashamed of how easily I was taken in by Violet. I shared so much information with her, never suspecting that she might use it for such devious purposes. My desire to visit Clovelly, the details of the upcoming art exhibition, even the estimated value of the paintings. I spoke of these things so freely, never imagining the consequences."

Watson said, "You mustn't blame yourself, Miss Davenport. Violet Brown is a master manipulator, skilled in the art of deception. Even the most discerning among us might have fallen victim to her charms."

Dorothy nodded. "Thank you for your understanding, Dr Watson. Because of what I'd done, I offered my resignation to Lord Cavendish. I felt I had failed in my duties, that I had put his lordship's reputation at risk through my own foolishness. But Lord Cavendish refused to accept my resignation. He said I was too important an employee for him to lose, and that we should put the past behind us."

Mrs Fairfax reached out and took her sister's hand, squeezing it gently in a gesture of support. "He recognises your worth, Dorothy, and he knows that you would never knowingly put his interests at risk."

Holmes said, "It may interest you to know, ladies, that Violet Brown and her associates have a long history of such thefts. Her husband and her brother have been her willing accomplices in a string of crimes that have spanned the length and breadth of the country. Until now, they have managed to evade capture, always staying one step ahead of the law."

Mrs Fairfax's eyes widened in surprise. "Truly, Mr Holmes? I had no idea that their criminal activities were so extensive."

Holmes continued, "And I must say, Mrs Fairfax, that if it were not for your concern over your sister's sudden departure, Violet Brown and her gang would have undoubtedly succeeded in yet another audacious theft. Your instincts were correct, and your actions set in motion the chain of events that led to their ultimate downfall."

Mrs Fairfax turned to her sister and said kindly, "You see, Dorothy, I was right to worry about you. I'll never stop worrying about you, no matter how far apart we live."

Dorothy smiled. "And I will always worry about you, my dear sister." She turned to Mr Holmes and Dr Watson. "Thank you again for all you've done. We will wish you farewell. My sister and I have a lot to catch up on."

As the door closed behind the departing sisters, Holmes and Watson settled back into their chairs, the room seeming somehow quieter in the wake of their guests' departure. For a moment, the only sound was the gentle crackling of the fire in the grate and the distant rumble of carriage wheels on the cobblestones outside.

"Well, Watson," Holmes said at last, breaking the contemplative silence, "I must say, this case has been a most interesting one. The machinations of the human mind never cease to amaze me, and Violet Brown's scheme was as devious as it was daring."

Watson nodded in agreement. "To think that she had been planning this theft for months, ingratiating herself with Miss Davenport and the other members of the book club, all the while gathering information that she could use to her advantage. It is a chilling reminder of the lengths to which some people will go in pursuit of their own selfish ends."

For a moment, the two men sat in companionable silence, each lost in their own thoughts. Then, Watson spoke again, his tone lighter, almost playful. "You know, Holmes, perhaps we should consider taking a holiday ourselves. Somewhere peaceful, perhaps by the sea."

Holmes chuckled, his eyes sparkling with amusement. "My dear Watson, I do believe you are becoming quite the romantic in your old age. A holiday by the sea, indeed! I can just imagine it now. You, lounging on the beach with a good book, while I am left to my own devices, searching for some mystery to solve amidst the tranquil countryside."

Watson laughed, shaking his head ruefully. "You are probably right, Holmes. Knowing you, you would likely stumble upon some nefarious plot or another. Perhaps it is best that we remain here in London, where the criminals are at least somewhat predictable."

Holmes smiled, leaning back in his chair with a contented sigh. "Ah, Watson, you know me too well. London is indeed where I belong, with its endless supply of puzzles and intrigues. But who knows? Perhaps one day, we shall find ourselves taking a holiday by the sea, chasing down some elusive criminal mastermind amidst the beaches and rocky cliffs."

Watson raised his teacup in a mock toast. "To future adventures, then, Holmes. Whether in London or further afield, I have no doubt that there will always be mysteries to solve and wrongs to right, as long as we are together."

Holmes raised his own cup in response, his expression one of genuine affection. "To future adventures, indeed, my dear Watson."

***

Read on for the first two chapters of the next book: Sherlock Holmes and The Baker Street Thefts

# Sherlock Holmes and The Baker Street Thefts – first two chapters

## Chapter 1

It was early afternoon, and inside 221B Baker Street, Sherlock Holmes was reading a mystery novel and occasionally shaking his head at the unlikely plot twists within the story. His companion, Dr John Watson, sat across from him, a newspaper on his lap. Dr Watson's eyes were closed and a light series of snores came from him.

The tranquil scene was suddenly shattered by the sound of hurried footsteps on the stairs, followed by a frantic knock at the door.

"Come in, Mrs Hudson," Holmes called out, recognising her knock.

Dr Watson snorted, opened his eyes and blinked. "What? What was that? What's going on?"

The door burst open, revealing their landlady, Mrs Hudson, her face flushed with agitation. "Mr Holmes, Dr Watson! Thank goodness you're both here."

Watson turned to look at their landlady. "Whatever is the matter, Mrs Hudson?"

"There are thefts taking place! Right here on Baker Street!" she exclaimed. "I've just heard about them from my neighbour, and I fear our home may be targeted next. Whatever shall we do?"

Holmes closed the book he was reading and placed it on the table next to him. "Thefts? Pray tell us more, Mrs Hudson. Please, sit down."

Mrs Hudson took a seat across from the two men. "My neighbour, Vera Wilkins, was telling me all about it. Apparently, there have been several incidents of valuable items going missing from various households on our very street."

"What sort of items?" Watson inquired.

"It seems to be jewellery," Mrs Hudson replied. "This morning, she saw the Thompsons on their doorstep discussing a missing brooch. They live further up the road, and on the opposite side. Anyway, Vera was walking past them on her way to the shops. Mrs Thompson was upset about something and her voice was quite loud. Well, Vera couldn't help but hear what they were saying, could she?"

Holmes smiled. "I suppose not. And what did Mr and Mrs Thompson have to say about this missing brooch?"

"Mr Thompson seemed to think it might have simply been misplaced," Mrs Hudson explained, "but Mrs Thompson was adamant it was on her dressing table because she always kept it there, but when she looked for it that morning, intending to wear it, it was gone. Mrs Thompson had searched her bedroom, but it was nowhere to be found."

Watson reached for his pocketbook and made a note about the incident.

"And then there's Mrs Henderson," Mrs Hudson continued, "who noticed a pearl necklace missing from her jewellery box a few days before."

"And how do you know about that?" Holmes asked.

Mrs Hudson replied, "Mrs Henderson told me. I was walking through the park yesterday as it was such a lovely day, and I saw Mrs Henderson sitting on a bench. She didn't look like her normal happy self at all. So, I asked if something was wrong. She told me about the missing necklace. She said she always keeps it in the jewellery box when she's not wearing it. But it's no longer there. She thinks she might have put it somewhere else for some reason, but now can't remember where she put it. She thinks she's losing her memory. Poor woman. I tried to be positive and said, these things turn up in unexpected places sometimes."

"That's true," Watson said. "I hope she finds that necklace soon."

Mrs Hudson's eyes narrowed. "The thing is, Dr Watson, I think it's been stolen, and I think Mrs Thompson's brooch has been stolen, too." She paused. "Someone else has noticed a missing piece of jewellery on this street, Mrs Baxter. She's lost some diamond earrings. And this happened last week, according to Vera, who is friends with Mrs Baxter's sister. Three missing items, all from people who live on this street. And they all occurred within the last few weeks. These are not coincidences. Not at all. And I know your feelings on coincidences, Mr Holmes."

"Indeed," Holmes replied. "I don't believe in them. Mrs Hudson. I agree these incidents are not coincidences, but evidence of something else taking place. Those missing items are small and easily transportable. This suggests a thief who is adept at moving swiftly and undetected."

"Precisely my thoughts, Mr Holmes," Mrs Hudson agreed. "I don't have many valuables, but the ones I have are very precious to me. And I know you two have items of value, too. With the thefts occurring so close to home, I'm worried that we may be the next targets."

"We shall take every precaution to ensure that does not happen," Holmes assured her. "Watson and I will look into this matter, and we will do so immediately."

Mrs Hudson sighed with relief. "I'm so glad to hear that, Mr Holmes, so very glad."

Holmes turned to Watson, a determined glint in his eye. "Watson, we shall pay a visit to the Thompsons and inquire about this missing brooch. It seems the most recent incident, and therefore, the one with the freshest trail to follow. Mrs Hudson, could you give me the house numbers of where Mrs Thompson and the other ladies live, please?"

"Of course." Mrs Hudson gave Holmes the required information.

As the two men prepared to depart, Mrs Hudson rose from her seat, a grateful smile on her face. "Thank you, gentlemen. I feel much better knowing you're on the case."

Holmes offered her a reassuring nod. "Have no fear, Mrs Hudson. We shall uncover the truth behind these thefts and ensure the perpetrator is brought to justice."

With that, the famous detective and his trusted companion set off, ready to make their investigations.

## Chapter 2

Minutes later, Sherlock Holmes and Dr Watson approached the ornate front door of the building where Mr and Mrs Thompson lived.

Holmes rapped on the door, and a few seconds passed before it swung open, revealing a young woman in a crisp maid's uniform.

"Good afternoon, sirs," she greeted, her tone polite but guarded. "How may I be of assistance?"

Holmes offered a warm smile. "Good day, miss. I am Sherlock Holmes, and this is my colleague, Dr John Watson. We're here to speak with Mrs Thompson regarding a rather delicate matter."

The maid's expression softened slightly, and she nodded. "Of course, Mr Holmes. Do come in." She ushered them inside, leading them through the foyer and into an elegantly appointed sitting room. "If you'll excuse me for a moment, I'll inform Mrs Thompson of your arrival."

As the maid departed, Watson leaned in closer to Holmes. "What are your initial observations, Holmes?"

Holmes scanned the room, taking in every detail. "The household appears well-kept, with no obvious signs of disarray or disturbance. I didn't see any signs of a forced entry on the main door or the front-facing windows. However, we mustn't draw any premature conclusions until we've spoken with Mrs Thompson herself."

Moments later, the maid returned, followed by a woman in her late fifties. Mrs Thompson was impeccably dressed, her greying hair styled in an elegant coiffure, and her demeanour exuded a sense of refinement and poise.

"Mr Holmes, Dr Watson," she greeted, her voice tinged with a hint of concern. "I understand you wished to speak with me about a delicate matter."

Holmes inclined his head respectfully. "We do, Mrs Thompson. We've been made aware of a recent incident involving a missing brooch belonging to yourself, and we were hoping you could provide us with more details."

Mrs Thompson's expression grew grave, and she motioned for them to take a seat. "Ah, yes, the brooch. A most distressing situation, I must say. It was a family heirloom, passed down through generations, and of immense sentimental value. I had placed it on my dressing table, as I always do after wearing it. I wished to wear it this morning, but when I looked for the brooch, it was gone."

Watson smiled gently, "Forgive me for asking, but are you certain it wasn't simply misplaced? These things do happen."

Mrs Thompson shook her head firmly. "I am meticulous in my habits, and I can assure you that the brooch was precisely where I always left it. I wear it most days and like to have it to hand when needed."

Holmes nodded. "And have you noticed any other items missing from your home, or any signs of a potential break-in?"

"Not that I'm aware of, Mr Holmes," Mrs Thompson replied. "The house appears undisturbed, and nothing else seems to be missing. It's as if the brooch simply vanished into thin air."

Holmes said, "Mrs Thompson, we've been informed that there have been other incidents of missing valuables on this very street. Are you aware of this?"

Mrs Thompson frowned. "No, I am not aware of that. Have these items vanished as mysteriously as mine?"

"It appears so," Holmes confirmed.

"May I ask, who has reported these incidents?" Mrs Thompson said.

"They haven't been reported as such," Holmes replied. "But the information has come to us via contacts. It seems Mrs Henderson has lost a pearl necklace, and Mrs Baxter has lost a pair of diamond earrings."

Mrs Thompson gasped. "No! But I am friends with those ladies. We meet almost every day for lunch. They never told me about their missing jewellery."

"Perhaps they thought the items had been misplaced and they would find them soon," Holmes offered.

Mrs Thompson nodded slowly. "Ah, yes, that could be the case. My husband thinks I've misplaced my brooch. We had quite the animated discussion on the doorstep this morning about it. I'm surprised the neighbours didn't hear us." Comprehension dawned on her face and she broke into a smile. "One of the neighbours did hear us, though, didn't she? I noticed Mrs Wilkins going by, and how her steps slowed when she passed our home. And Mrs Wilkins is a good friend of your lovely landlady. Now, I understand how you know about my brooch."

Holmes bowed his head a little. "Yes, people are prone to discuss their neighbour's lives. This information was passed to us with honest intentions, and not as malicious gossip, I assure you."

Mrs Thompson waved a hand dismissively. "I can see that, Mr Holmes. And I'm glad the information was passed to you. Can I assume you will look into this matter on my behalf?"

"Of course," Holmes replied. "We will investigate this mystery thoroughly, and we will find the person behind it. You have my word. Furthermore, we will do our utmost to reunite you with your brooch.

Mrs Thompson clasped her hands together, her eyes shining with relief. "Oh, Mr Holmes, I cannot begin to express my gratitude. This brooch means the world to me, and the thought of losing it forever is simply unbearable."

Holmes rose from his seat, offering Mrs Thompson a reassuring smile. "We shall leave no stone unturned in our investigation. If any further information comes to your mind about this mystery, no matter how insignificant it may seem, I implore you to share it with us."

Mrs Thompson nodded, her expression resolute. "Of course, Mr Holmes. Anything to aid in the recovery of my beloved brooch."

"One more thing before we go. May we speak with your maid, the one who answered the door? She may have noticed someone unusual hanging around recently. Perhaps someone who was showing an interest in your home, and those of your neighbours."

Mrs Thompson said, "Matilda? Oh, of course. Yes, please do speak to her. She'll be in the kitchen at this time of the day."

"Thank you, we will seek her out. How long has Matilda worked for you?" Holmes asked.

Mrs Thompson smiled. "Ten years. She's like part of the family. I don't know what I'd do without her."

*** 

Click the title to read the rest of Sherlock Holmes and The Baker Street Thefts

# The Sherlock Holmes series

Book 1 –  Sherlock Holmes and The Missing Portrait

Book 2 – Sherlock Holmes and The Haunted Museum

Book 3 – Sherlock Holmes and The Hasty Holiday

Book 4 – Sherlock Holmes and The Baker Street Thefts

Book 5 – Sherlock Holmes and The Lamplighter's Mystery

Book 6 – Sherlock Holmes and The Vanishing Act

Book 7 – Sherlock Holmes and The Cat Burglar

Book 8 – Sherlock Holmes and The Unwanted Client

Book 9 – Sherlock Holmes and The Other Detective

Book 10 – Sherlock Holmes and Dr Watson's Disappearance

# A note from the author

For as long as I can remember, I have loved reading mystery books. It started with Enid Blyton's Famous Five, and The Secret Seven. As I got older, I progressed to Agatha Christie books, and of course, Sir Arthur Conan Doyle's Sherlock Holmes.

I love the characters of Sherlock Holmes and Dr Watson, and the Victorian era that the stories are set in. It seemed only natural that one day, I would write some of my own Sherlock stories. I love creating new mysteries for Mr Holmes, and his trusty companion, Dr John Watson. It's not just the era itself that seems to ignite ideas within me; it's also the characters who were around at that time, and the lives they led.

This story has been checked for errors, but if you see anything we have missed and you'd like to let us know about them, please email mabel@mabelswift.com

You can hear about my new releases by signing up to my newsletter  As a thank you for subscribing, I will send you a free short story: Sherlock Holmes and The Curious Clock.

If you'd like to contact me, you can get in touch via mabel@mabelswift.com I'd be delighted to hear from you.

Best wishes

Mabel